THE GREAT GRAND CANYON TIME TRAIN

SUSAN LOWELL
ILLUSTRATED BY
JOHN W. SHROADES

RIO CHICO
Books for Children

CONDUCT
800
11
CANYON

The twins' tickets were shining silver, just like the train.

"So," Sam said to the conductor, "if this is the Grand Canyon Railway—"

"—does it really go *all the way*?" said Rosie.

Sam and Rosie often had exactly the same idea. Or else they had exactly opposite ideas. And then—look out!

"Oh, yes," smiled the conductor.

But the twins' parents said, "Whoa!"

They often thought alike, too, but if thoughts had colors, parent ideas were brown, and twin ideas were rainbow-striped.

"The train goes all the way *to* the Grand Canyon," explained Mom.

"And stops," said Dad. "Then we get out. No train could go all the way down."

"Why not?" asked Rosie.

"The canyon is too big," said Dad.

"And DEEP," said Mom. "Just wait. You'll see!"

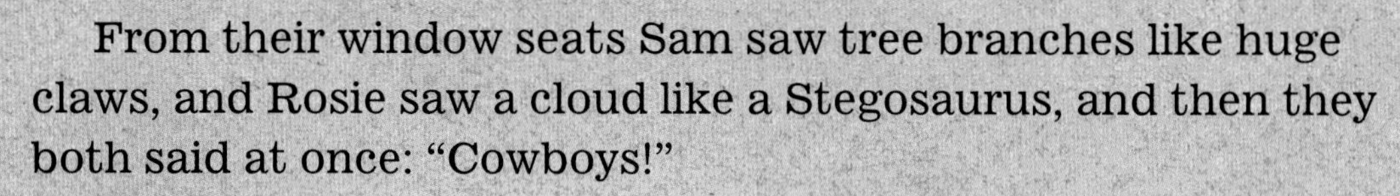

From their window seats Sam saw tree branches like huge claws, and Rosie saw a cloud like a Stegosaurus, and then they both said at once: "Cowboys!"

"Where?" said their parents. But the cowboys were gone.

"Maybe they galloped away," said the twins.

"Maybe just a reflection in the window," said Mom.

Just as the train finally reached the Grand Canyon Depot, it happened again.

"Look!" cried the twins. "A one-armed man with a funny beard!"

"And suspenders," said Sam.

"You two!" said Mom fondly.

"Great imaginations!" said Dad.

"And," said Rosie, "a lady in a long black dress—"

"With a white apron," interrupted Sam.

"And a tray," Rosie finished.

Their parents smiled and shook their heads.

"*She* waved," Rosie whispered, and Sam nodded. "*He* winked," he said.

The station swarmed with excited children, newly arrived from somewhere else, who laughed and jumped as they greeted their families. Many of these children had streaks of chocolate on their faces.

And they all wore suspenders.

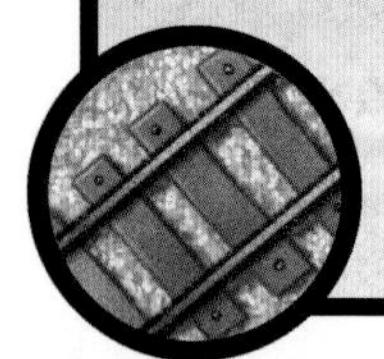

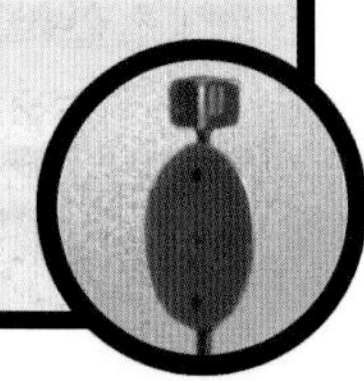

GRAND
GREAT GRAND CANYON TIME
ROLLER COASTER
Zigs, Zags, Chills, and
ENTER HERE

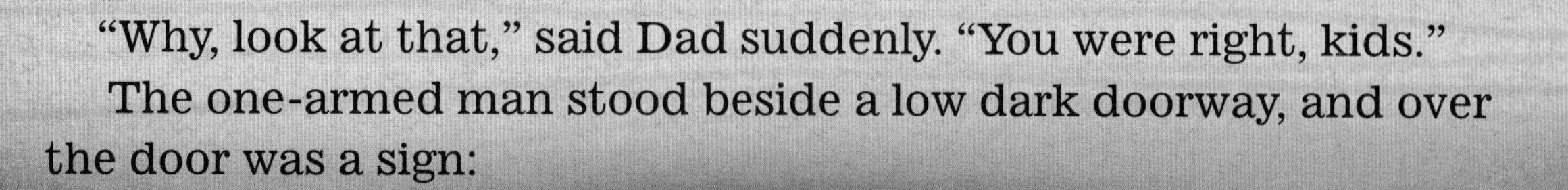

"Why, look at that," said Dad suddenly. "You were right, kids."

The one-armed man stood beside a low dark doorway, and over the door was a sign:

GREAT GRAND CANYON TIME TRAIN
ROLLER COASTER SUPREME
Zigs, Zags, Chills, and Thrills!
ENTER HERE

"Oh, can we go, please, please?" cried Rosie and Sam.

"What about the Grand Canyon?" said their parents.

"Do you still have your train tickets?" asked the one-armed man. "All you need are six minutes and a silver ticket." He turned to Mom and Dad. "It's very educational! Allow me to introduce myself."

He clicked his heels together and bowed. "Major John Wesley Powell, former director, U.S. Geological Survey. I will be their guide. The seats are rather small," he added, "so bigger people usually drink coffee or go to the visitor center instead."

Just what parents liked, thought Sam and Rosie.

"Please!" they said again.

"Well, all right," said their parents. "Geology. Fine. Meet back here in six minutes."

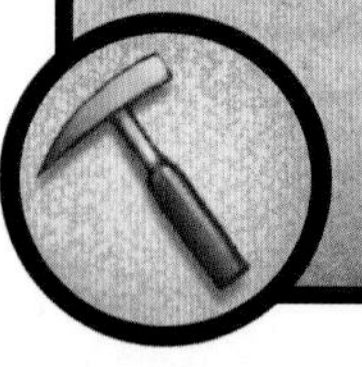

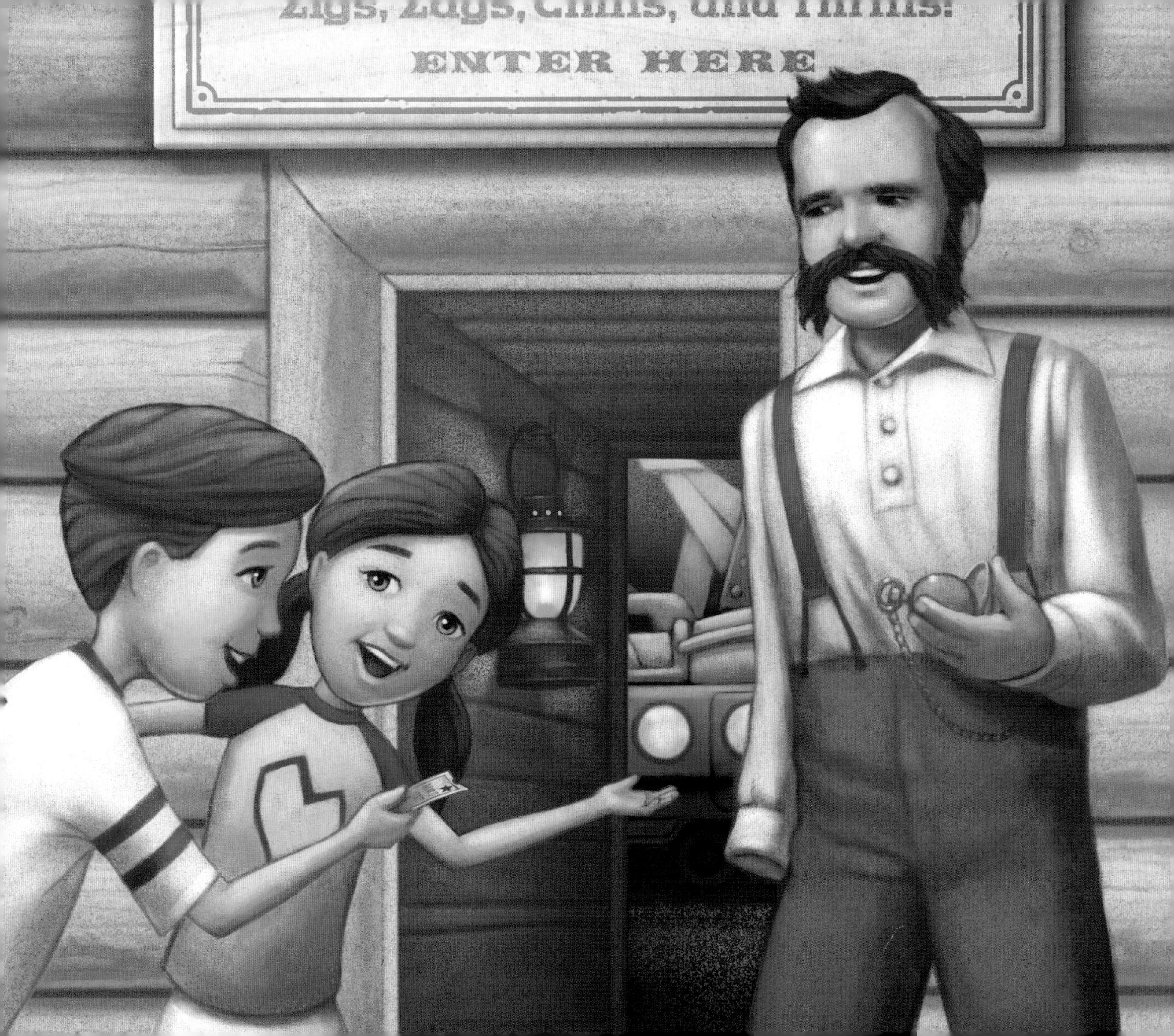
ENTER HERE

FOSSILS

"Quick!" said Major Powell, hurrying the twins through the door. "We've got a long way to go."

The Time Train looked like an armor-plated swordfish with wheels. . .and wings. . .and dials.

"Are those clocks?" Rosie whispered.

The train was already stuffed with chattering children, but the twins managed to squeeze inside. Criss-crossed on each seat was a beautiful pair of suspenders.

"Explorers!" Major Powell shouted. "All aboard! Buckle your suspenders!"

Instantly the Time Train took off. The racket was awful. They seemed to be drilling a tunnel straight through the earth.

Then **THUNK!** The train stopped. Stepping smoothly down the aisle came three young ladies in long black dresses and ruffled white aprons. Each one carried a tray and wore a fancy pin that said:

"In the great kitchen of the universe," said Major Powell, "we find three kinds of rocks."

On the first Harvey Girl's tray, the children saw ingredients for cookies. "The first kind of rock, ladies and gentlemen, is sedimentary," said Major Powell, "meaning mixtures of particles, like cookie dough."

"If," he went on, "we stir and bake that mixture, *sedimentary* rocks change into the second kind of rock, *metamorphic.*" The second Harvey Girl held out her tray, and all the children cried, "Cookies!"

"What's the third kind?" asked the twins.

"Hotter than baked," said Major Powell. "Melted, deep underground. Think volcanoes. *Igneous.*"

"Fudge!" said the third Harvey Girl.

PRESENT
PRESENT
FLOUR
SUGAR
VANILLA
BROWN SUGAR

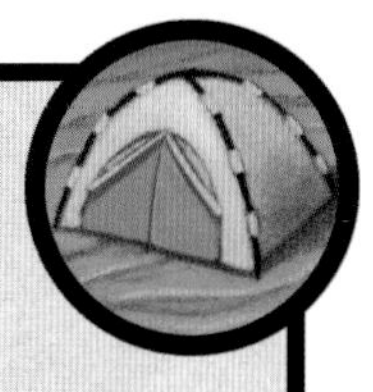

Then, **CRASH!**

The train leaped out of the rock and teetered on the South Rim of the Grand Canyon.

"Ohhh!" the children gasped.

"Yep," said the Major. "It's a pretty grand old ditch! Now, kids, look out there. Forget cookies. What do you see?"

And they all shouted together, "Layer cake!"

"Right you are," said Major Powell. "Hang on tight, now, because we're going doooooooooooooown!"

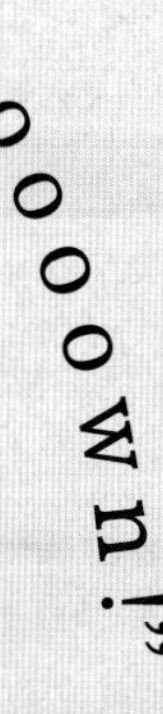

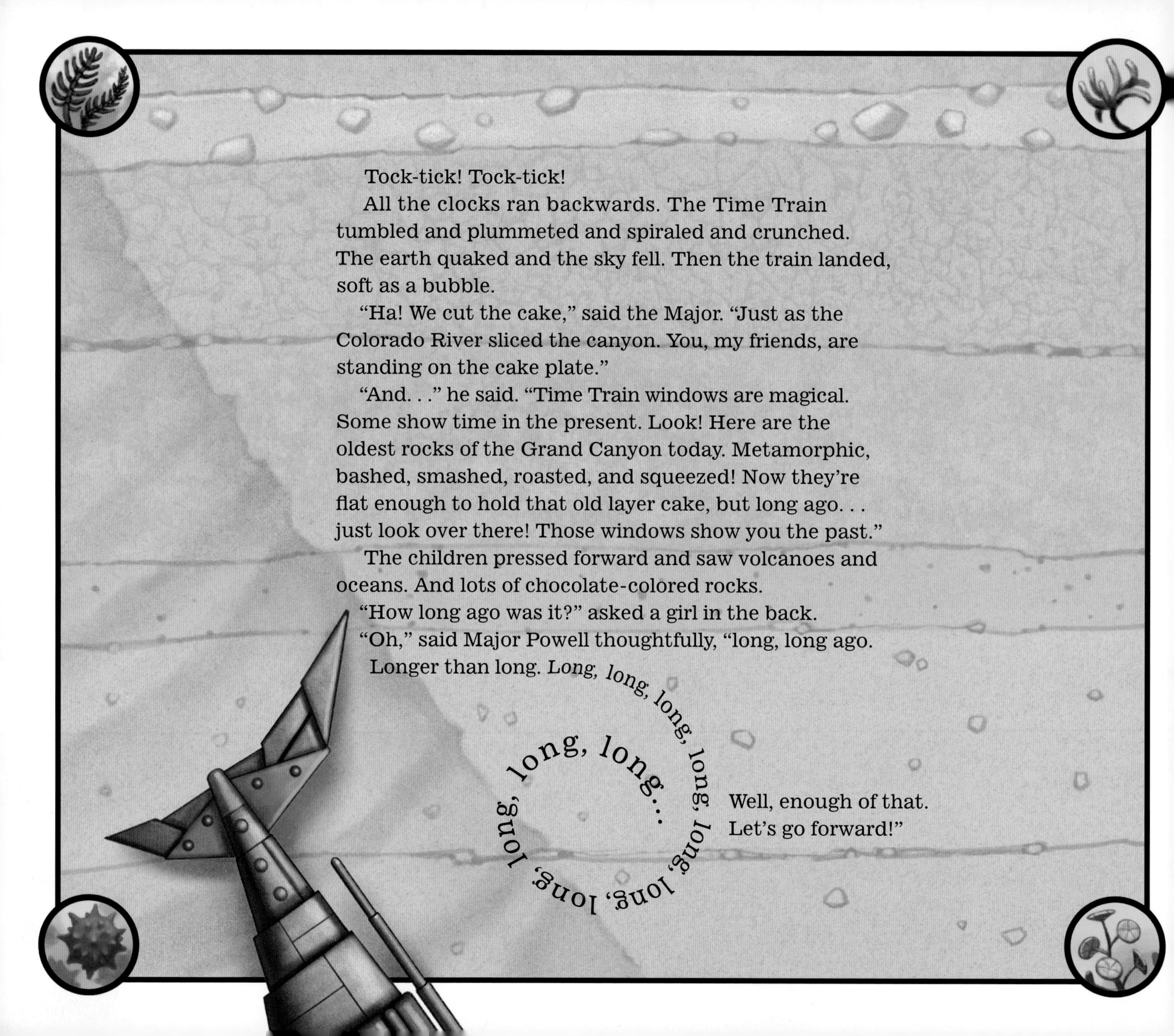

Tock-tick! Tock-tick!

All the clocks ran backwards. The Time Train tumbled and plummeted and spiraled and crunched. The earth quaked and the sky fell. Then the train landed, soft as a bubble.

"Ha! We cut the cake," said the Major. "Just as the Colorado River sliced the canyon. You, my friends, are standing on the cake plate."

"And. . ." he said. "Time Train windows are magical. Some show time in the present. Look! Here are the oldest rocks of the Grand Canyon today. Metamorphic, bashed, smashed, roasted, and squeezed! Now they're flat enough to hold that old layer cake, but long ago. . . just look over there! Those windows show you the past."

The children pressed forward and saw volcanoes and oceans. And lots of chocolate-colored rocks.

"How long ago was it?" asked a girl in the back.

"Oh," said Major Powell thoughtfully, "long, long ago. Longer than long. *Long,* long, long, long, long, long, long, long, long, long. . . Well, enough of that. Let's go forward!"

CAMBRIAN
PRESENT

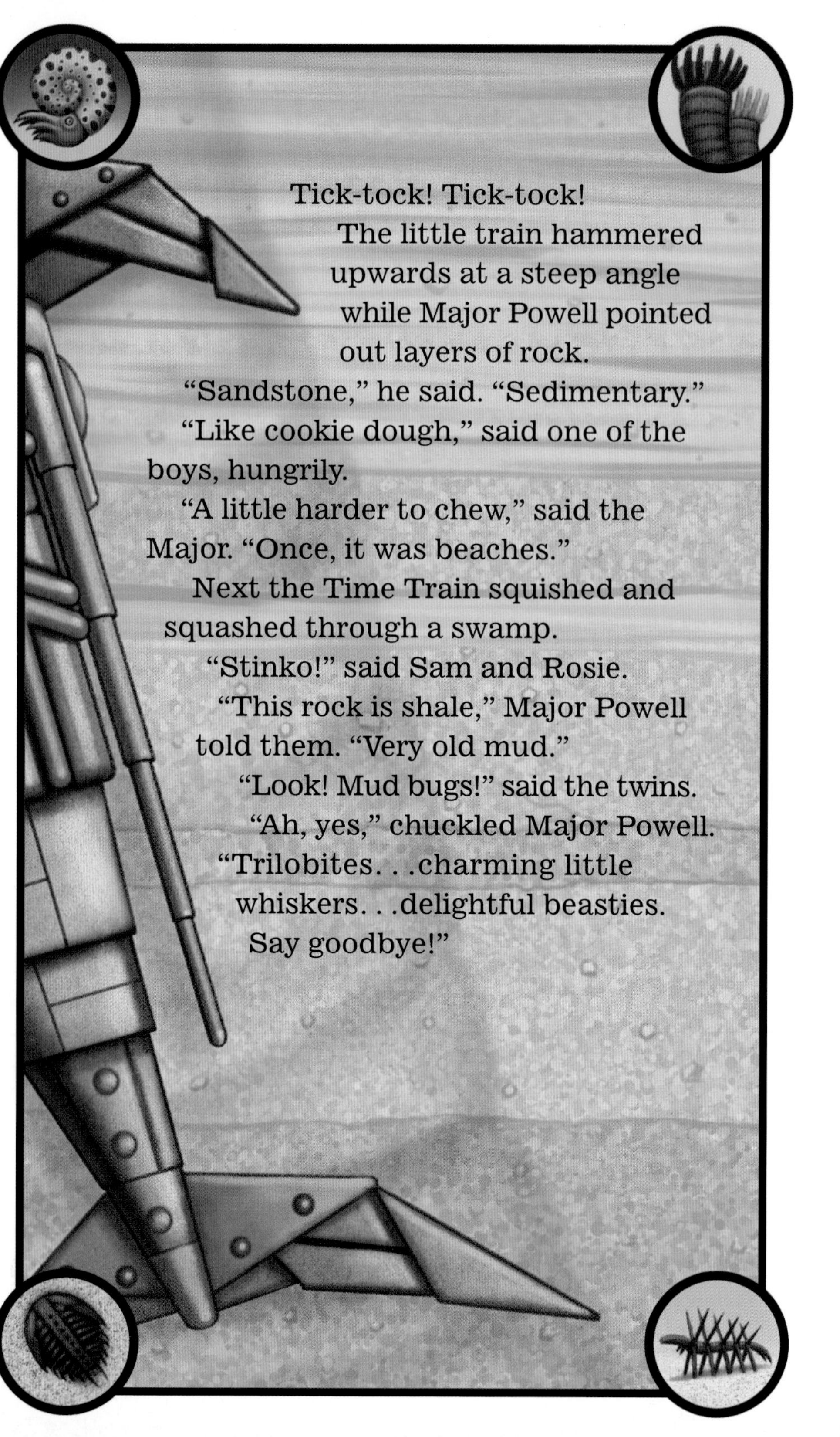

Tick-tock! Tick-tock!

The little train hammered upwards at a steep angle while Major Powell pointed out layers of rock.

"Sandstone," he said. "Sedimentary."

"Like cookie dough," said one of the boys, hungrily.

"A little harder to chew," said the Major. "Once, it was beaches."

Next the Time Train squished and squashed through a swamp.

"Stinko!" said Sam and Rosie.

"This rock is shale," Major Powell told them. "Very old mud."

"Look! Mud bugs!" said the twins.

"Ah, yes," chuckled Major Powell. "Trilobites. . .charming little whiskers. . .delightful beasties. Say goodbye!"

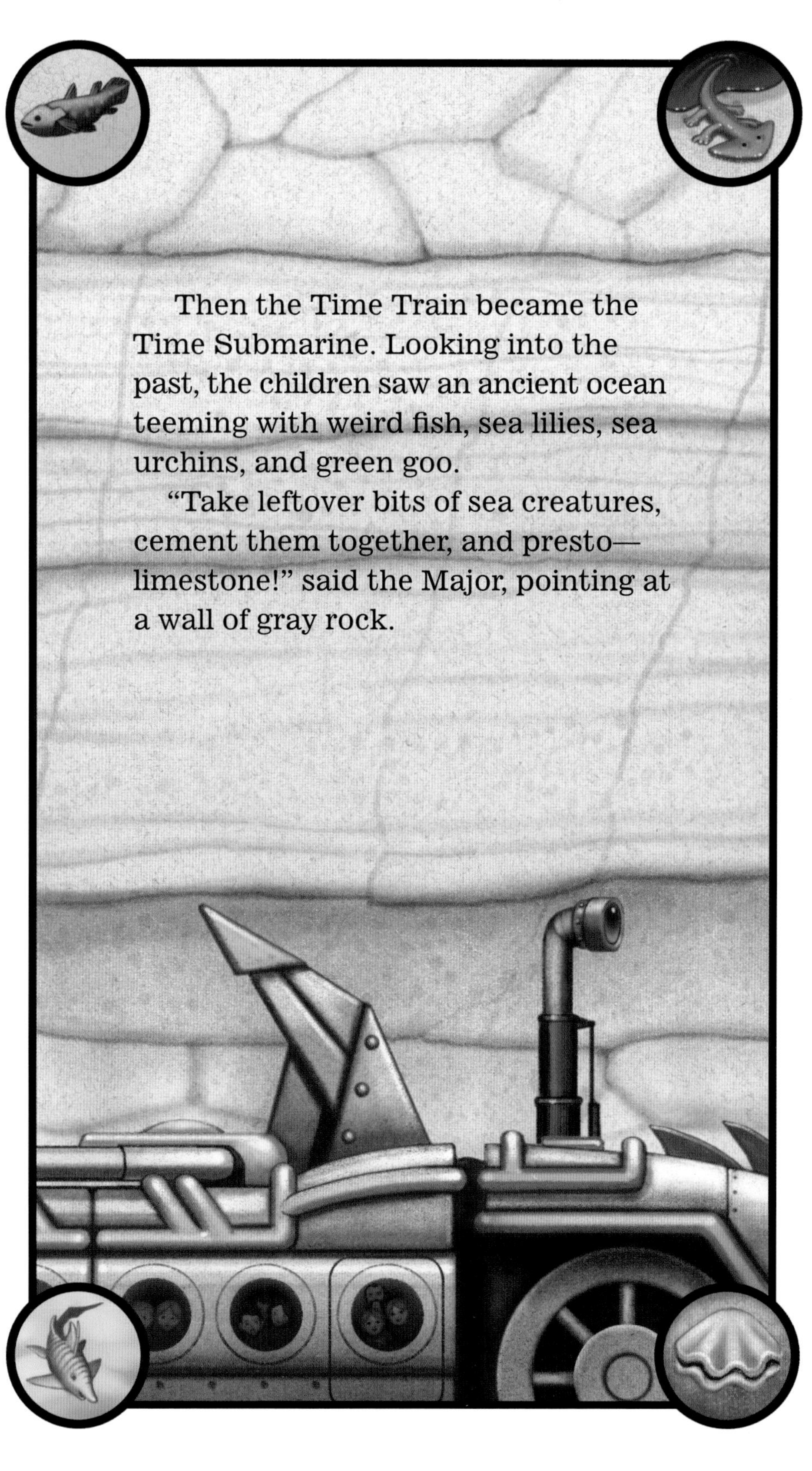

Then the Time Train became the Time Submarine. Looking into the past, the children saw an ancient ocean teeming with weird fish, sea lilies, sea urchins, and green goo.

"Take leftover bits of sea creatures, cement them together, and presto—limestone!" said the Major, pointing at a wall of gray rock.

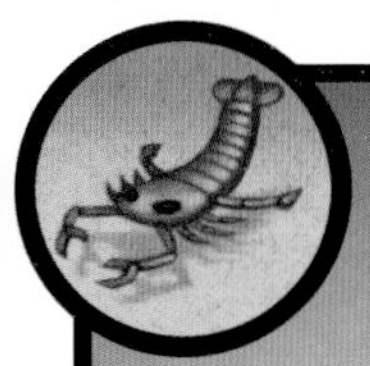

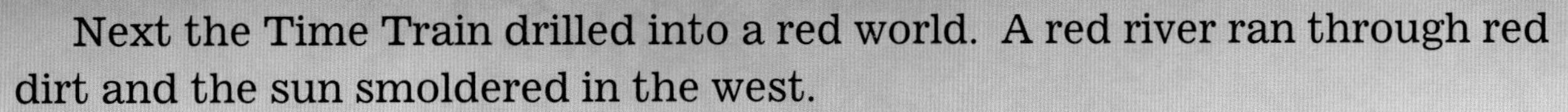

Next the Time Train drilled into a red world. A red river ran through red dirt and the sun smoldered in the west.

"Dragon—" said Rosie.

"Flies!" said Sam. "And ferns."

But then the sand began to blow—and blow—until the Time Tractor was crawling through a sand sea. Giant scorpions peeked through the windows, and the children saw reptile tracks in the sand.

After the sandstorm the Time Ship cruised across a tropical lagoon like blue glass above pearly fish and rainbow coral reefs. The Harvey Girls served refreshments.

"Well, explorers, we're almost home again," said Major Powell. "There's time for one more adventure, though. Who wants to take the Dinosaur Detour?"

Everyone yelled, "WE DO!"

"Then we'll have to fly out of the canyon," he said. "Ten, nine, eight…"

When the clouds cleared, the children looked down.

"It's a real Stegosaurus!" shouted Rosie.

"No," cried Sam. "Anklysaurus!"

"You're wrong!"

"No, you are!"

"Bonehead!"

"Duckbill!"

"Allosaurus breath!"

"Gigantosaurus gas!"

50 MILLION
years ago

15,000
years ago

10,000
years ago

The more they fought, the faster the Time Rocket flew, past giant sloths, miniature horses, woolly mammoths, and a beautiful Native American girl in a leather dress. Last came a stout cowboy on horseback, wearing glasses and a short bristly mustache.

"Good to see you, Mr. President!" Major Powell called.

THUD! Back in the train station, the twins thanked Major Powell, who gave them one final wink.

"Well, how was it?" said Mom and Dad, who were loaded with hats, sunscreen, binoculars, guidebooks, and cameras.

The twins looked at each other and laughed. Then they each turned a huge cartwheel.

"GRRRANNND—" shouted Rosie.

"DERFUL!" yelled Sam.

"You two!" said their parents, looking at them fondly. "Let's go!"

And so they did.

GIFT
SHOP

Now that we know the way, we're going to make our very own...
Grand—
No, GRANDERFUL.

No, GRANDEST Canyon...
Time travel...
Guide book...
Sam + Rosie's Book

Just for kids!
Whoo-hoo!

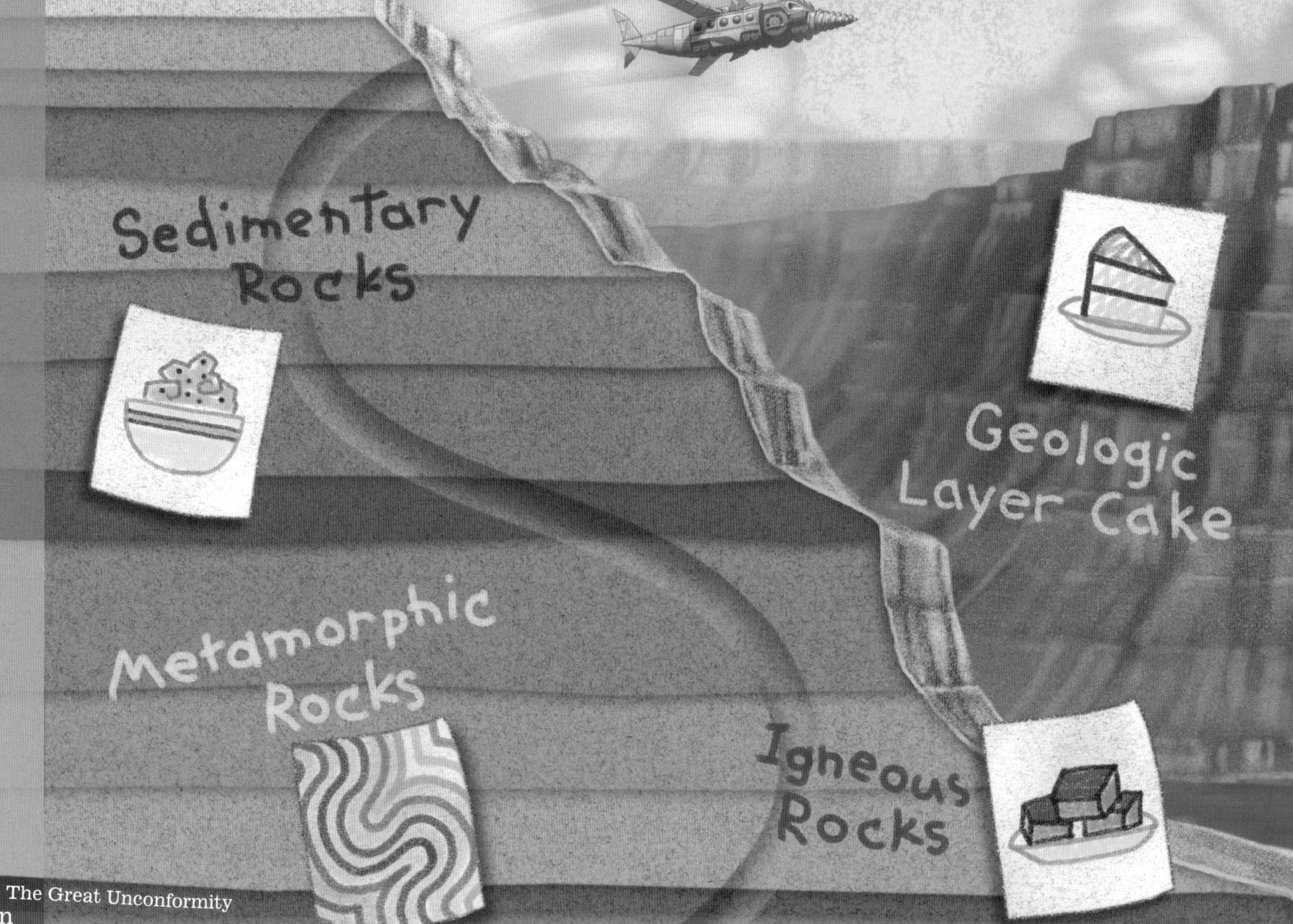
Late Paleozoic
Middle Paleozoic
Early Paleozoic
Precambrian
The Great Unconformity
Sedimentary Rocks
Metamorphic Rocks
Igneous Rocks
Geologic Layer Cake

We'll go by the fastest, easiest way—even better than the Time Train.
IMAGINATION!

Here we go...
Way, way, way deep in time!

I'll make pictures.
I'll take notes.

Dino Detour
Dragonfly!
Fish!
Trilobite!
We're making a book! Want a peek?
Turn the page!

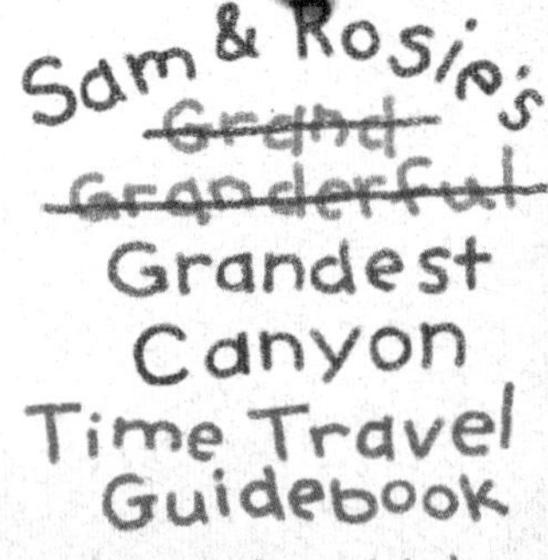

No dinosaur fossils in the Grand Canyon. Why? Because those rocks probably washed away. But you can find GREAT dinosaurs on "detours" nearby.

1869–Major John Wesley Powell led the first modern explorers through the Grand Canyon by boat.

1908–President Theodore Roosevelt made the Grand Canyon a National Monument.

Many ancient Native Americans lived at the Grand Canyon–and many modern ones still do.

1901–the first train arrived at the Grand Canyon, and they still come today.

Tourists loved Harvey hotels and restaurants. Judy Garland played a Harvey Girl waitress in a movie!

To Ross
—S.L.

To my dad
—J.W.S.

Rio Chico is an imprint of Rio Nuevo Publishers®
P. O. Box 5250, Tucson, AZ 85703-0250
(520)623-9558, www.rionuevo.com

Editorial: Theresa Howell
Design: David Jenney

First Impression 2011
ISBN: 978-1-933855-63-9

Composed in the United States of America

Printed in China.

6 5 4 3 2 14 15 16

Library of Congress Cataloging-in-Publication Data

Lowell, Susan, 1950-
The great Grand Canyon Time Train / by Susan Lowell; illustrations by John W. Shroades.
p. cm.
Summary: Two twins go on a magical, geological trip back in time to the bottom of the Grand Canyon.
ISBN-13: 978-1-933855-63-9 (hardcover : alk. paper)
ISBN-10: 1-933855-63-0 (hardcover : alk. paper)
1. Grand Canyon (Ariz.)—Juvenile fiction. [1. Grand Canyon (Ariz.)—Fiction. 2. Time travel—Fiction. 3. Geology—Fiction. 4. Brothers and sisters—Fiction. 5. Twins—Fiction.] I. Shroades, John, ill. II. Title.
PZ7.L9648Gr 2011
[E]—dc22
2011006693